The Ants Go Marching One By One

Frankie O'Connor
Illustrated by Nicole Groot

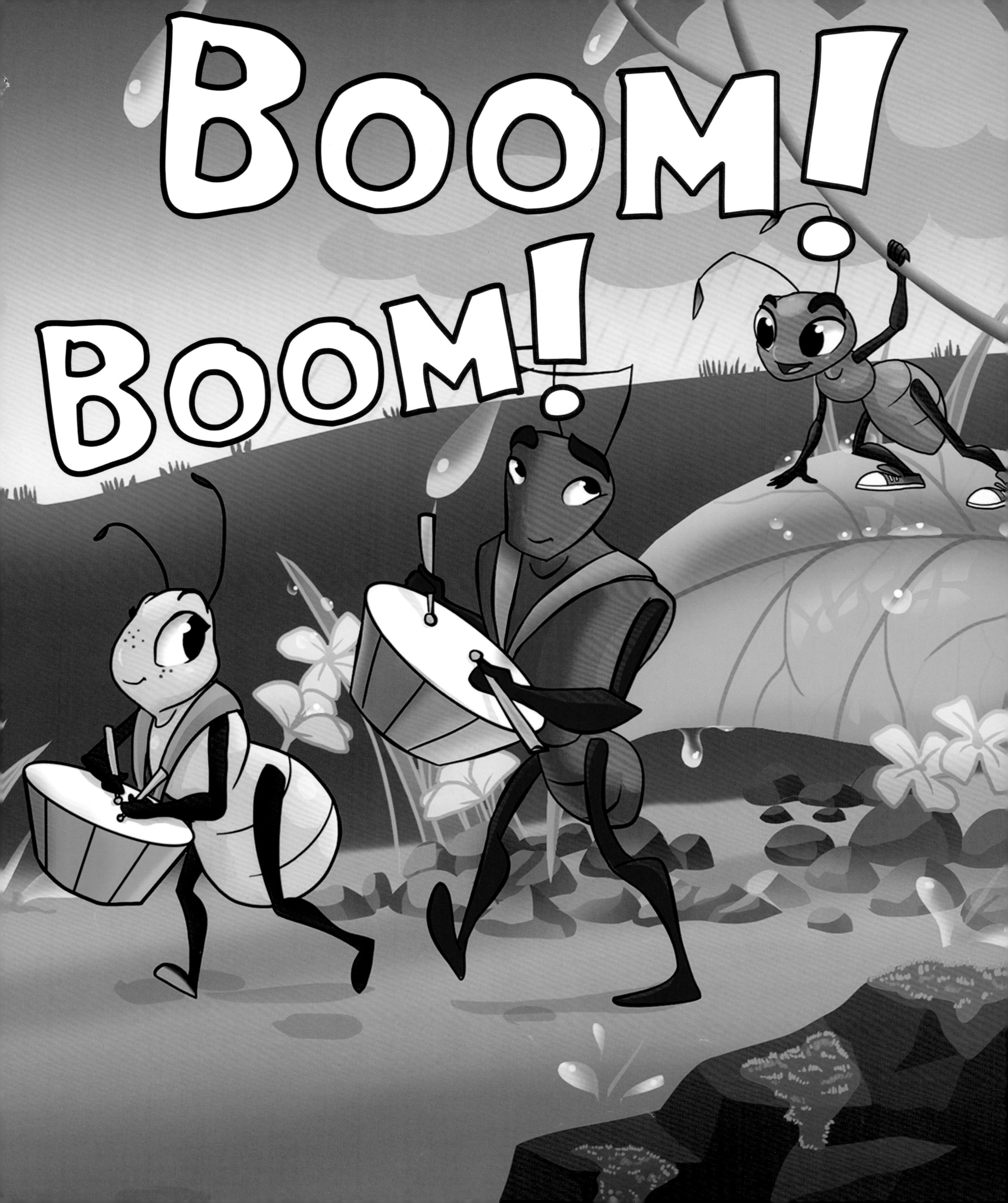
BOOM!
BOOM!

The little one stops to have some fun,
and they all go marching down,
to the ground,
to get out of the rain.

BOOM!

BOOM!

BOOM!

BOOM!

The little one stops to tie his shoe,
and they all go marching down,
to the ground,
to get out of the rain.

BOOM!
BOOM!
BOOM!
BOOM!

The ants go marching three by three,
HURRAH! HURRAH!
The ants go marching three by three,
HURRAH! HURRAH!
The ants go marching three by three,

The little one stops to water ski,
and they all go marching down,
to the ground,
to get out of the rain.

BOOM!

BOOM! BOOM!

BOOM!

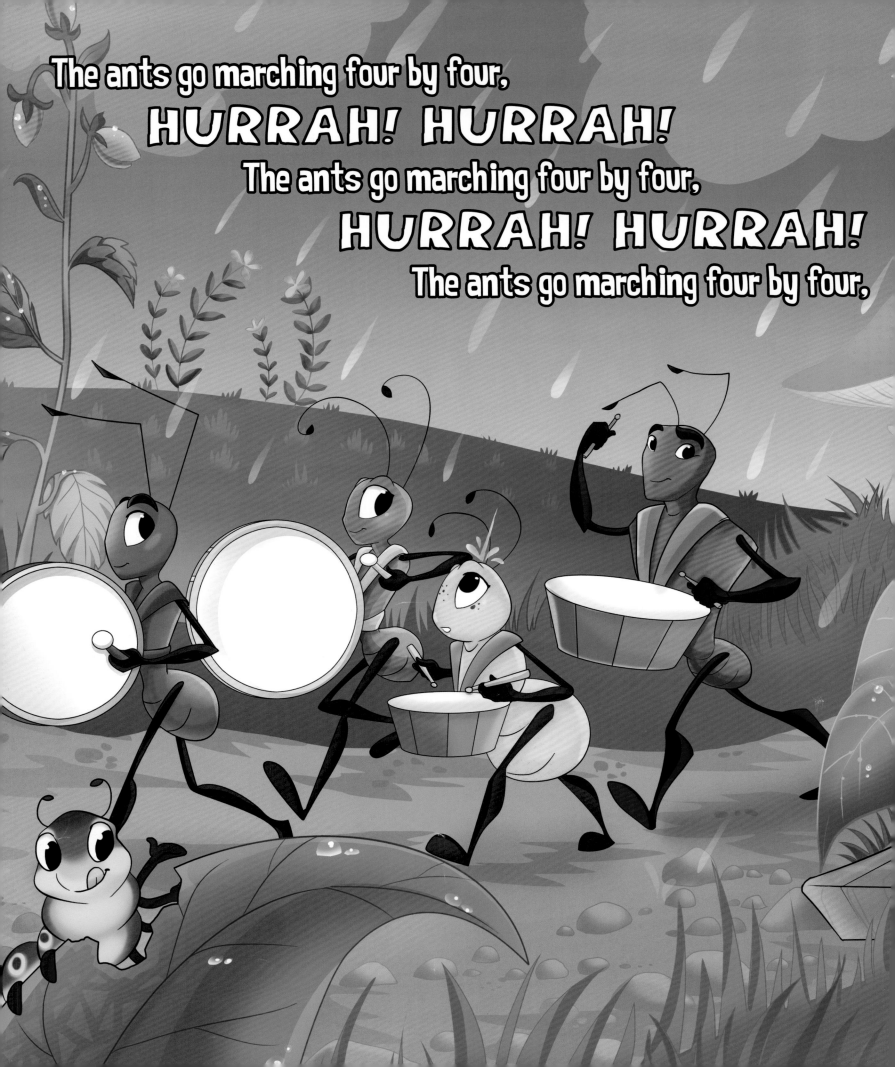

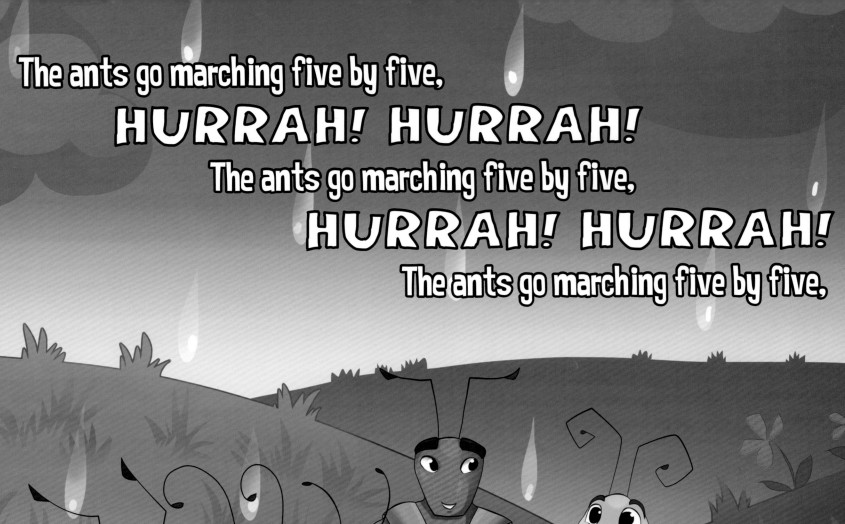

The ants go marching five by five,
HURRAH! HURRAH!
The ants go marching five by five,
HURRAH! HURRAH!
The ants go marching five by five,

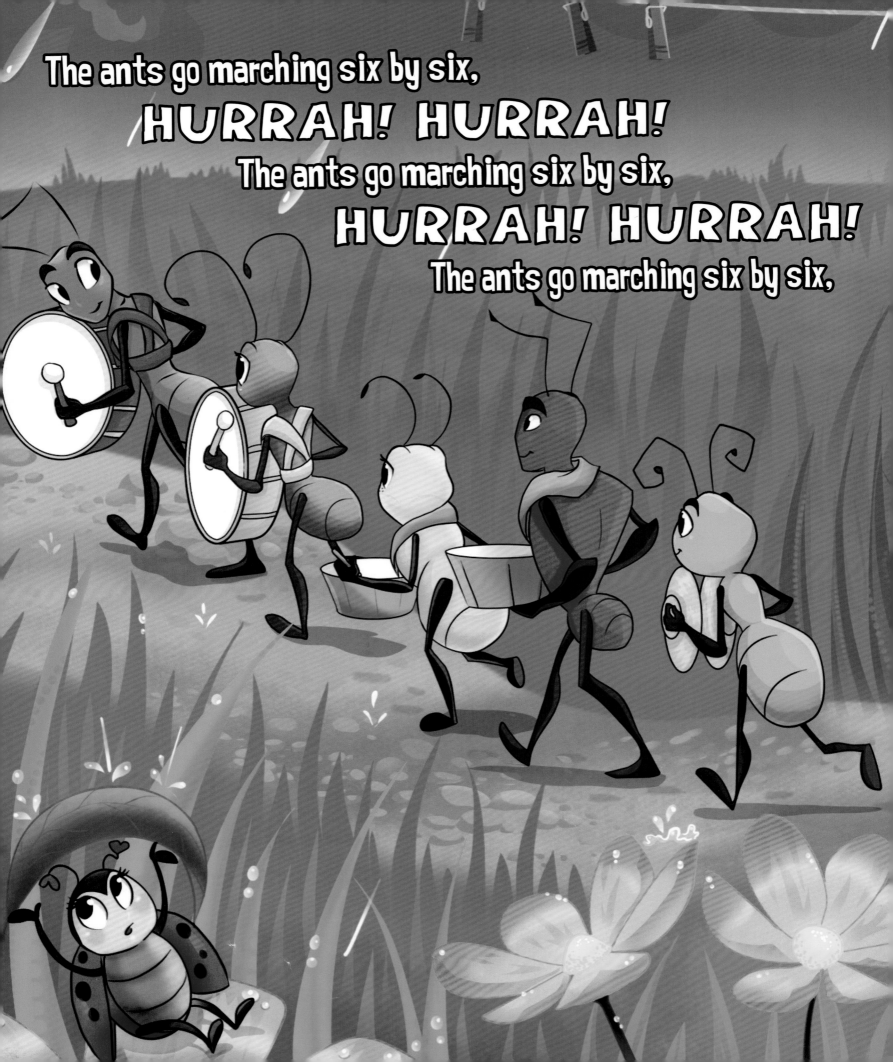

The little one stops to do some tricks,
and they all go marching down,
to the ground,
to get out of the rain.

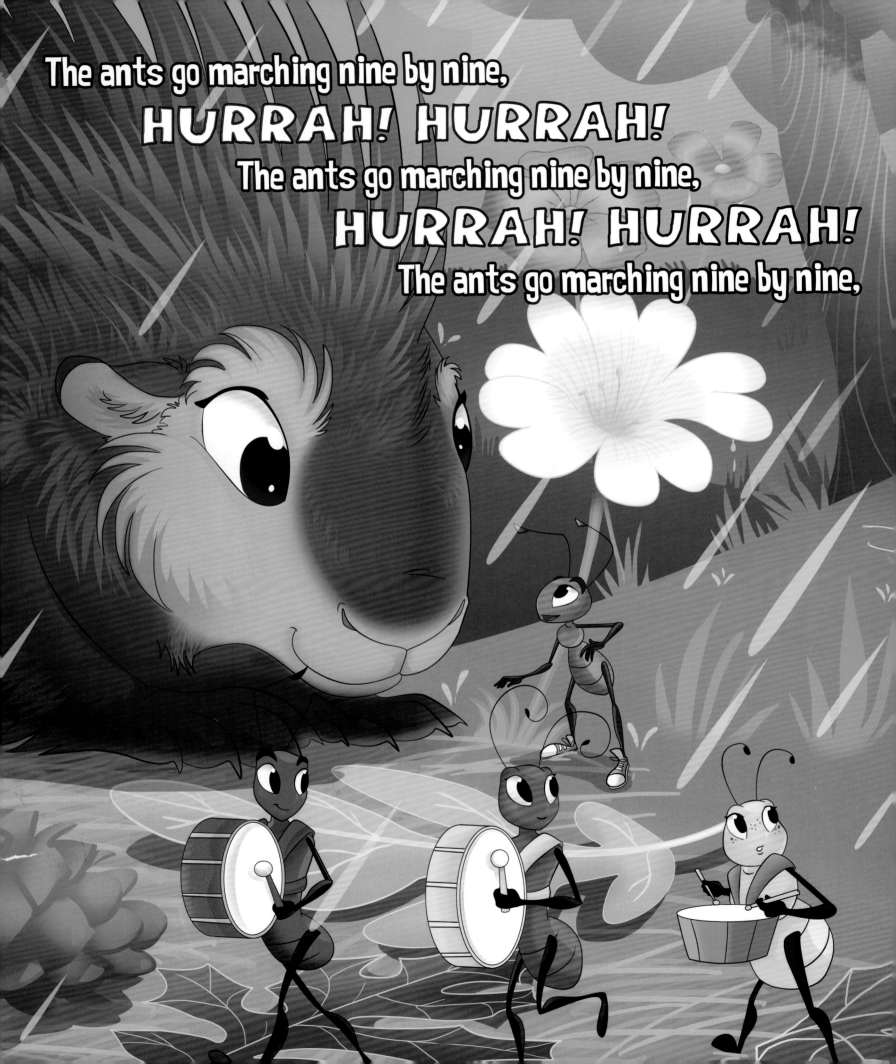

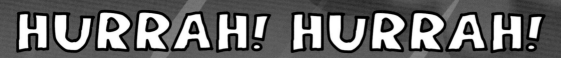

HURRAH! HURRAH!
The ants go marching ten by ten,
The little one stops to say...

Boom! Boom! Boom! Boom!